For Parker, Rowan, and Hayes, who keep me outside well below zero.

May you always choose joy through life's adventures!

ISBN 13: 978-1-63489-415-9

Library of Congress Catalog Number has been applied for.
Printed in the United States of America
First Printing: 2021

25 24 23 22 21   5 4 3 2 1

Cover and interior design by Mayfly Design

Wise Ink Creative Publishing
807 Broadway St NE, Suite 46, Minneapolis, MN, 55413

To order, visit www.itascabooks.com or call 1-800-901-3480. Reseller discounts available.

Winter, You Wonder

Written by

PERRIS DEPPA

Illustrated by

RAQUEL MARTÍN

Do stars get cold on a wind-chilled night,
or does the moon open his arms to snuggle them tight?

Do snowflakes whisper as
they fall to the ground,
or does the wind simply swish
them around and around?

Do snowbanks compete
to be tallest in height,
or are they merely
a show of a
snowplow's
great might?

Oh what a wonderful wintery world!

Does a snowball excite at the chance to take flight,
or wish to be made into an igloo built right?

Does a cold frozen lake scare the fish below,
or is the world above the surface beyond what they know?

Do icicles know the power they hold?

Perhaps only we know they're sharp blades of cold.

Oh what a wonderful wintery world!

Do snowmen wish for an
orange carrot nose,

or yearn for a scarf
and some warm
winter clothes?

Does a pine tree stay cozy under dazzling, bright lights,
or fear having its branches wrapped a bit too tight?

Is a blizzard a grand, lively party of snow,

or a snowflake reunion—
now how would we know?!

Oh what a wonderful wintery world!

Does the sun start her day melting snowdrifts below,
or bask in their beautiful white morning glow?

Do the critters of winter delight in its calm,
or count down the days 'til next summer's balm?

Does a rink keep the secrets of its skaters untold,

or share them with puddles as new seasons unfold?

Oh what a wonderful wintery world!

Ignite your imagination, embrace the cold.

And when you do . . .

Find joy in discovering winter's wonder anew!